altair design

Developed by Ensor Holiday / Pantheon Books

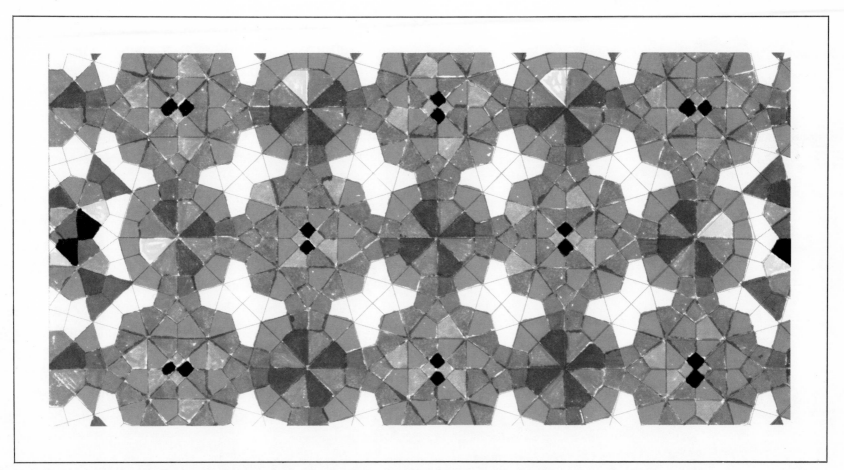

have you ever been awed by the complexity of a maze, or traced with your fingers the lace grillwork of an old iron gate, or studied the patterns emerging from a tile floor? Have you ever wondered—however briefly—about mankind's perennial search for harmonious lines, shapes, and patterns? Have you ever considered that throughout history and around the world certain designs occur with infinite variation? Have you ever asked yourself whether there might be something common to them all? The last question in particular has always intrigued Ensor Holiday, the man who created ALTAIR DESIGN.

Holiday, a British biologist whose hobby is geometry, was injured several years ago in a car accident and while recovering began to explore this idea: Is there a common mathematical basis for certain geometric designs? A week's project turned into two years of consuming activity. With the help of a computer he proceeded to develop a number of linear forms that in turn generated specific designs which encompass innumerable patterns. The eight designs printed in this book—in multiple reproductions—are the result of his efforts and offer a point of departure into an exciting world of personal creativity.

A fascination with Altair designs is something that all people can share. Like Altair, the star of mariners, Altair designs guide the imagination of man through a maze of lines. They enable individuals to shape on paper the images stirred in their minds. No two people are alike and for that reason no two people will see the same shapes, forms, or patterns hidden in these designs. Altair designs are open to all kinds of interpretation: abstract, realistic, and decorative, which can be expressed through a personal choice of color and shapes. The designs help to develop personal and original responses to forms and colors, and the individual will find pleasure in repeating the patterns in symmetrical and decorative ways.

In short, ALTAIR DESIGN is so intensely stimulating because it touches on the basic relationship between what we see and what we experience. Whether we discover a pentagon or a five-pointed star, a maze of streets or a tartan plaid, we are making a personal, meaningful choice. Whether we experiment alone or in a group the results will be different and satisfying, and the process will furnish many hours of pleasure for a variety of people of all ages.

Outline or fill in spaces, emphasize some lines and ignore others completely, add what suggests itself—the structure of the design will make it all fit together. The mechanical process is simple, the tools required easy to get: felt-tipped pens, magic markers, crayons, colored pencils, pastels, or water colors.

ALTAIR DESIGN is an exercise in form, shape, and color. Both children and adults will develop their sensitivity in these areas. They will be identifying geometric shapes, imagining pictures, combining colors in ingenious ways, and discovering the pleasure of creative involvement.

More complicated uses are also possible: the craftsman looking for design ideas can use the patterns as a springboard for working out a woodblock or a motif for a ceramic. ALTAIR DESIGN provides marvelous, imaginative possibilities for mosaics, appliqués, patchwork, embroidery, and needlepoint. Metal could be etched, fabric could be hand-printed, in forms evolved from these patterns. A window, or perhaps a covering for a light, might be painted in transparent glazes—again in a design evolved from these patterns—to create a glowing bit of beauty. The possibilities are fascinating and endless.

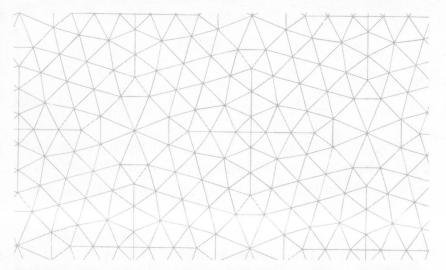

Design 1: A series of octagons (squares with their corners clipped off) awaits you. Turn the sheet and as you look along the diagonal you may find lemon shapes or even precious gems. Narrow your focus and you may discover a hectagon (seven-sided figure), or a Maltese cross inside an octagon—although you may choose to see that as an eight-pointed star or a square with concave sides. Perhaps some irregular shapes will appear and disappear, like a cut-glass bowl, a crown, a whiskered cat, balloons, or little, old-fashioned, peaked-roof houses.

Design 3: Perhaps you will find a plaid, or straight and narrow streets. If you're in the mood for a mathematical puzzle you might like to find out how many squares there are in this design. And a more difficult challenge: What is the smallest part of the design that includes all the lines needed to make the repeat pattern?

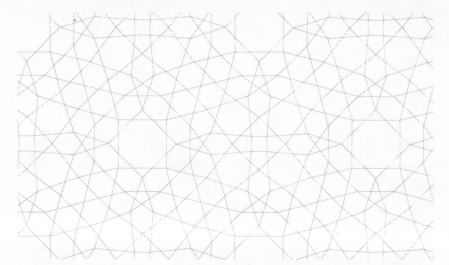

Design 2: Some people have discovered overlapping plates or raindrop ripples in a pool; others have found sausages in this same design. Or perhaps you will find a street grid if you rotate it. This design is rich in geometric shapes: squares, five-pointed stars (the ancient mystic pentagram), and six-pointed Stars of David that are formed by two overlapping, reversed, equilateral triangles. Will you find arrowheads, kites, Gothic windows, and crosses, or perhaps other figures of your imagination?

Design 4: Because this design consists entirely of polygons with radial lines, it is marvelous for spotting shapes—a game everyone loves. And its crisp texture makes for an interesting interplay of colors.

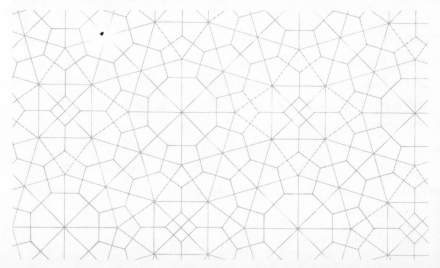

Design 5: An impression of depth on a flat surface provides enormous fascination. Opportunities for tiling with curious shapes exist and the tiling effect can be heightened by covering the complete sheet of paper with the basic pattern. By using mirrors or folding the sheets one can find lines of symmetry in this design.

Design 6: This is Design 4 without the radial lines but with the polygons. Perhaps for some people it will be a map; if so here's a puzzle question: How few colors are needed so that neighboring countries do not have the same color? Usually the answer is four, but three might just be possible here.

Designs 7 and 8: These are variations on Designs 1 and 2. By this time you have evolved your own ideas and these designs will be added fuel to keep the excitement going.

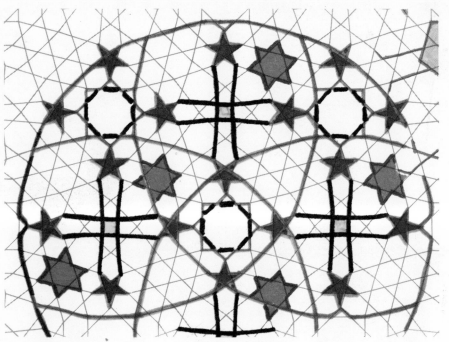

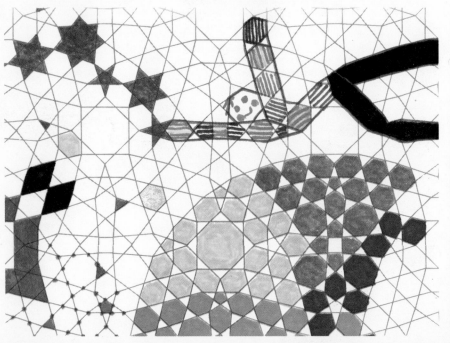
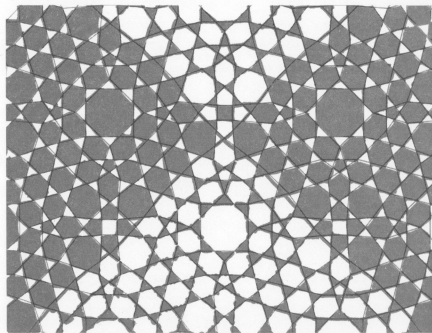

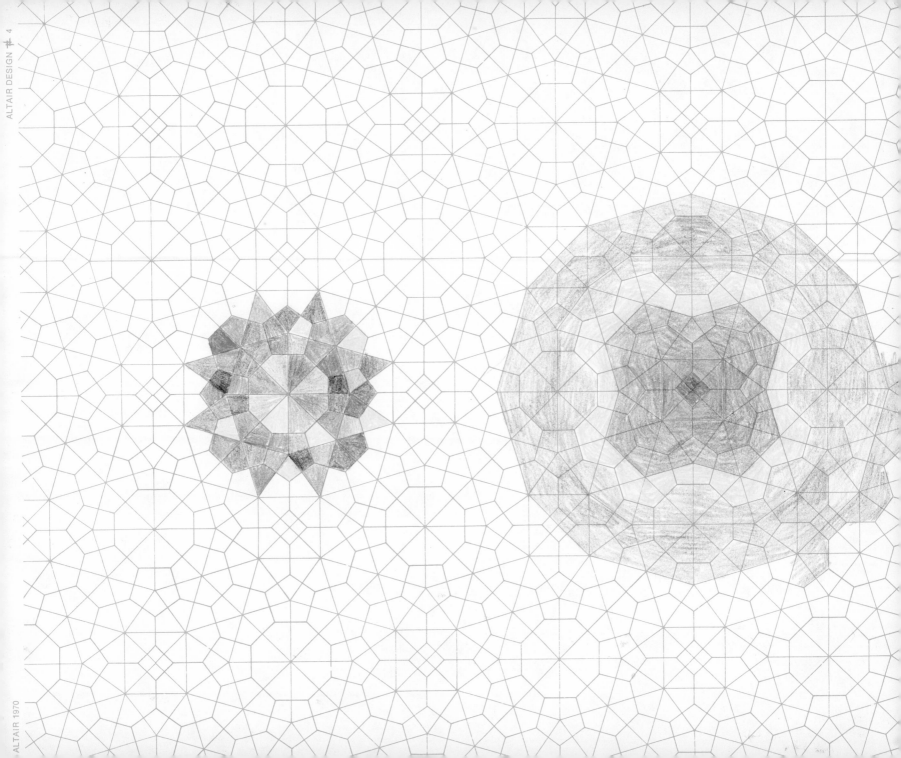

ALTAIR DESIGN # 4

ALTAIR 1970

ALTAIR 1970

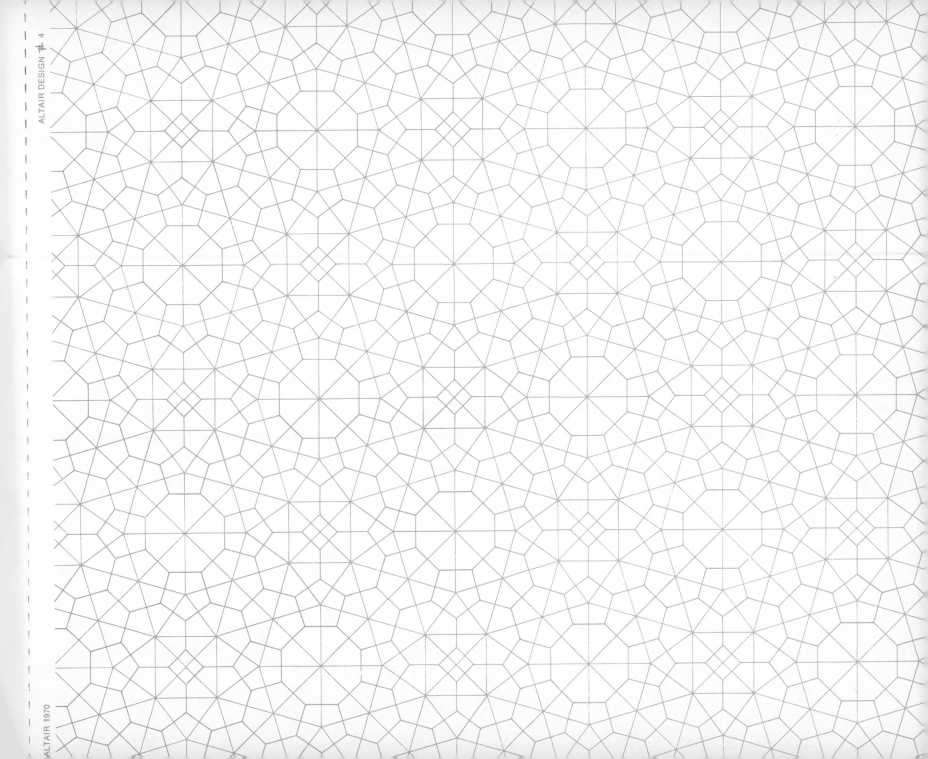

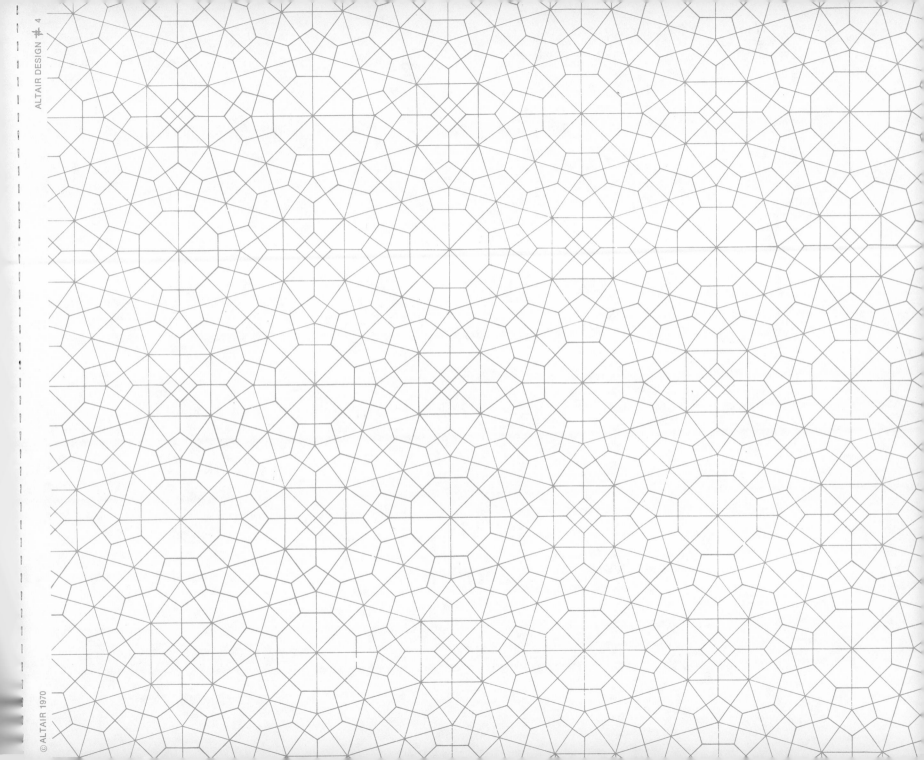